the Plumber

by ALLAN AHLBERG

with pictures by
JOE WRIGHT

PUFFIN

'FIN BOOKS

y the Penguin Group
rand, London WC2R 0RL, England
lson Street, New York, New York 10014, USA
Penguin Books Australia Ltd, 250 Camberwell Road, Camberwell, Victoria 3124, Australia
Penguin Books Canada Ltd, 10 Alcorn Avenue, Toronto, Ontario, Canada M4V 3B2
Penguin Books India (P) Ltd, 11 Community Centre, Panchsheel Park, New Delhi – 110 017, India
Penguin Group (NZ), cnr Airborne and Rosedale Roads, Albany, Auckland 1310, New Zealand
Penguin Books (South Africa) (Pty) Ltd, 24 Sturdee Avenue, Rosebank 2196, South Africa

Penguin Books Ltd, Registered Offices: 80 Strand, London WC2R 0RL, England

First published by Viking 1980
Published in Puffin Books 1980
36   37   38   39   40   41   42   43   44   45   46

Text copyright © Allan Ahlberg, 1980
Illustrations copyright © Joe Wright, 1980
All rights reserved

Set in Century Schoolbook by Filmtype Services Limited, Scarborough
Manufactured in China

British Library Cataloguing in Publication Data
A CIP catalogue record for this books is available from the British Library

ISBN–13: 978–0–14031–238–6

If ever a plumber was needed
in the town,
the people said, "Send for
Mrs Plug!"

When Mrs Plug was sent for,
Mrs Plug came.
Mr Plug came too.
He was the plumber's mate.
Miss Plug and Master Plug
also came.
They were the plumber's babies.

Mrs Plug had a useful bag.

It had a saw, a hammer,
a spanner, a pair of pliers,

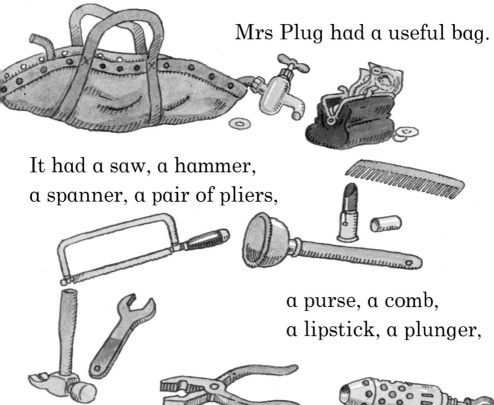

a purse, a comb,
a lipstick, a plunger,

a blow-lamp
and a few other things in it.

One night there was some trouble
in a lady's bathroom.
A plumber was needed.
The neighbours said,
"Send for Mrs Plug!"

Send for Mrs Plug!

When Mrs Plug was sent for,
Mrs Plug came.
But Mr Plug did not come.
He had to put the little Plugs
to bed.

Mrs Plug got on with the job.
The lady gave her a cup of tea.
When she had finished
the lady gave her some money.
Mrs Plug set off home.

On the way,
a terrible thing happened.
Mrs Plug saw a robber.

He was robbing a rich man
in the street.
The robber saw Mrs Plug.
He wanted to rob her too.

"What's in that bag?" he said.
"There's a comb," said Mrs Plug.
"I will have that!" said
the robber.
"And a lipstick," said Mrs Plug.
"I will have that!" said
the robber.
"And . . . a . . . blow-lamp!"
said Mrs Plug.

Mrs Plug chased the robber
with the blow-lamp.
She burnt his bottom.
"Wow!" the robber shouted.
And he ran off.

"That's a useful bag,"
the rich man said.
Then he said thank you to Mrs Plug
and gave her a reward.
It was four tickets for a voyage
round the world.
"My wife and I were going to take
the children," he said.
"But we can take them next week."

Mrs Plug went home.
She told Mr Plug about the robber
and the rich man.
She showed him the reward.
"You did very well, my dear,"
said Mr Plug.
He gave her a cup of tea
and a kiss.

The next day Mrs and Mr Plug
got ready for the world voyage.
They packed their cases.
They asked a neighbour
to take care of the cat.
They put a note out for
the milkman.

Then off they went.
Mr Plug carried the cases
and the little Plugs.
Mrs Plug carried the useful bag.

The voyage began.
The Plug family had a happy time.
They saw icebergs in the
northern seas.
They saw flying fish in the
southern seas.
They had dinner at the
captain's table.
They danced on deck under
the stars.

Then, one night,
a terrible thing happened.
There was a storm.

The ship hit a rock.
A hole appeared in its side.
The water poured in.

"Help, help!" the people shouted.
They ran about
in their nighties and pyjamas.
"We will all be drowned!"
The captain looked at the hole.
"I think we need a plumber," he said.
"Send for Mrs Plug!"
When Mrs Plug was sent for,
Mrs Plug came.
So did Mr Plug and the little Plugs.
So did the useful bag.

Mrs Plug got on with the job.
She used the spanner and
the hammer.
She used the pair of pliers
and the blow-lamp.
Mr Plug helped her.
They both got soaking wet.
They mended the hole!

All the people gathered round.
"Three cheers for the plumber
and the plumber's mate!"
the captain said.
"Three cheers for the
plumber's babies!"
"Three cheers for the
plumber's bag!"

The next night there was a big
celebration party.
The Plug family had dinner
at the captain's table.
Mrs and Mr Plug danced on deck
under the stars.

The little Plugs stayed
with the captain.
They sat on his knee.
They played with his gold watch
and his beard.

Suddenly the captain felt his knee
getting wet.
He looked at the little Plugs.
"I think one of you needs
a plumber," he said.
"Send for Mrs Plug!"

The End